Too Hot!

Written by Clare Helen Welsh

Illustrated by Laura Proietti

Collins

Fern is in the pool.

She is too hot.

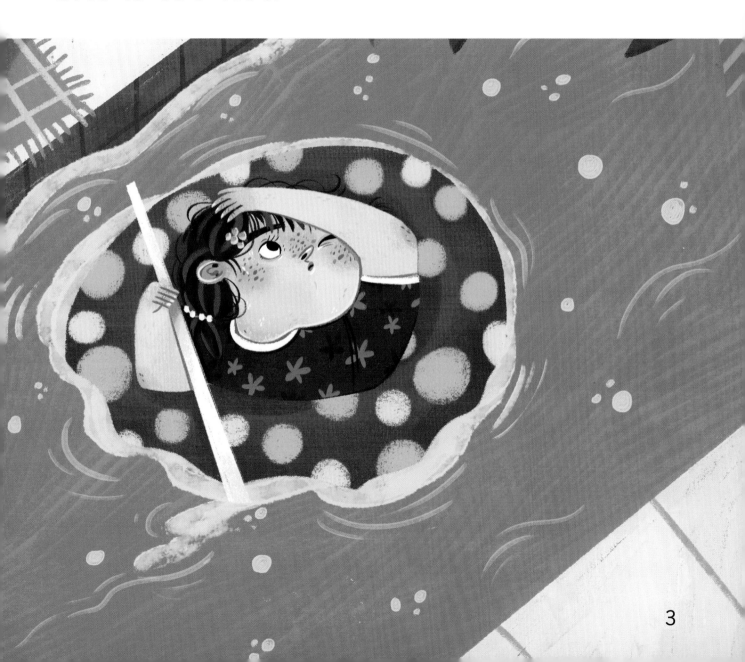

Matt yells, "Put on that cool sunhat."

5

A sudden turn and Fern sees a fin.

Fern runs into the deep bit.

She yells, "Shark! Shark!"

Wait. That is not a shark.

It is Matt.

"Too cool," moans Fern.

13

How Fern feels

After reading

Letters and Sounds: Phase 3

Word count: 58

Focus phonemes: /ai/ /ee/ /oa/ /oo/ /ar/ /ur/ /ow/ /er/

Common exception words: the, she, put, and, into, are, you

Curriculum links: Understanding the world; Personal, social and emotional development

Early learning goals: Reading: read and understand simple sentences; use phonic knowledge to decode regular words and read them aloud accurately; read some common irregular words

Developing fluency

- Your child may enjoy hearing you read the book.
- Take turns to read a page with your child. Demonstrate how to use a different voice for Matt and Fern. Encourage your child to read words or sentences that end with an exclamation mark with expression (despair on page 5; surprise/horror on pages 7 and 9).

Phonic practice

- Focus on words that contain two letters that make one sound. Check your child remembers that the common exception word **you** has an unusual /oo/ spelling, then ask them to sound out the following words:

Fern	turn	shark
too	pool	moans
you	now	deep

- Ask them to point to the two letters in each word that make one sound.

Extending vocabulary

- Ask your child to suggest words or phrases that mean the opposite to these:

| hot (*cold/cool*) | sudden (*slow/gradual*) | now (*later*) |
| yells (*whispers*) | runs (*walks slowly*) | |

Comprehension

- Turn to pages 14 and 15 and ask your child to describe how Fern feels in each picture, and why.